Visit us on the Web!
Seussville.com
rhcbooks.com

Educators and librarians, for a variety of teaching tools, visit us at RHTeachersLibrarians.com

Library of Congress Cataloging-in-Publication Data is available upon request.
ISBN 978-0-593-12797-1 (trade) — ISBN 978-0-593-12798-8 (lib. bdg.)

Printed in the United States of America
10 9 8 7 6 5 4 3 2 1
First Edition

IF I HAD YOUR VOTE

by **the Cat in the Hat**
with a little help from **Alastair Heim**

illustrated by **Tom Brannon**

BEGINNER BOOKS®
A Division of Random House

If I had your vote,
oh, the things I could do!
Oh, the things I could do
with a YES vote from you!

If I had your vote,
and if I were in charge,
I would make a few changes.
Some small and some large.

If I had your vote,
and a fun, fun, FUN staff
(and not just a staff
but a STAFF AND A HALF),

I would have my fun staff
fill the fridge with fun foods,
like hot dogs and cakes,
that make fun-feeling moods!

If I had your vote,
I would really prefer
this office to be
far more OVAL-ER-ER.

Thing One and Thing Two
would know just what to do
to square up this room
and RE-OVAL it through.

If I had your vote,
I would smile and smile
and sit very still
for a very long while.

The painters would paint me,
from morning till night,
to get every inch
of my SMILER just right.

If I had your vote,
I would sign all these bills
with ink and a pen
made from Stick-U-Pine quills.

These bills would become laws,
and those laws, with some luck,
would now and for always
stay stick-ity stuck.

If I had your vote,
I could be on TV
with ALL of these pointy things
pointing at me.

I would be in your house!
You could all see my face!

You could all see my face
even way out in space!

If I had your vote,
I would take all these books
and sort them by smell
and hook them on hooks,
so that all you would need
is your nose, beak, or snout
to sniff out a title
and check a book out.

I wonder what THIS
kind of book is about. . . .

If I had your vote,

I would paint this whole place.

These cases.

These vases.

These boots
and their laces

and all these tall walls
with their UN-FUNNY faces.

But as for THIS room,
I would leave it alone.
That hat on his head
looks A LOT like my own!

If I had your vote
and these plates
and old bowls,
for fun, I would put them
on top of these poles
and twirl them
and swirl them
around and around
until they stop spinning
and fall to the ground.

But, no need to panic
or worry, you see . . .
the NEW ones I pick
will be perfect for me!

If I had your vote,
I would meet other leaders
who happen, like me,
to be quite messy eaters.

Oh, how we would eat!
We would eat, eat, eat, eat!
With our SKORKS and our FLOONS
and our hands and our feet.

If I had your vote,
I would plant far more flowers
and trim these high hedges
for hours and hours,

then shower the flowers
with water I take
from this SPLISHY
and SPLASHY
and FISHY-FREE lake.

If I had your vote
and some almost-hatched eggs
(with SHELLS up on top
and the bottom half, LEGS),
those long-legged eggs
would NOT be a batch
of eggs you could catch
before they all hatch.

If I had your vote,
every night in the sky
would look like it looks
on the Fourth of July.

KA-BOOMS of all colors,
like pink, blue, and red,
would spark up the dark
in the sky overhead . . .

. . . and right at the end,
I would send up a SOCK-IT.
A SOCK-IT the size
of a space shuttle rocket!

The SOCK-IT would soar
and KA-BOOM in the sky,
then socks of all sizes
would fall from up high.

If I had your vote,
I could hire a crew,
a CLEAN-IT-ALL crew
that would clean this house through.

Thing One would wipe windows.

Thing Two would scrub chairs.

And Little Cat A

would SHAM-POOZLE the stairs.

Then Little Cat B,
all the way to Cat Z,
would sweep every speckle
of dirt they could see.

With one final touch-up
from Little Cat Q,
this not-so-new house
would look newer than new.

If I had your vote,

that is what I would do!

The country would LOVE me, I think. . . .

How about you?